WALT DISNEY'S Pinocchio

GROLIER
B O O K S

Hello! My name is Jiminy Cricket. I never used to believe in the wishing star. Let me tell you why I changed my mind.

It all started one night in a wood-carver's shop. The shop was owned by a kind man named Geppetto. Geppetto had made a puppet out of wood. It looked just like a little boy.

Geppetto lived with his cat, Figaro, and his fish, Cleo.
"Just a little more paint and he's finished," Geppetto
told them. He painted on a smile. Then the old man
smiled, too.

"I have just the name for you," Geppetto said to the
puppet. "Pinocchio!"

Soon Geppetto was climbing into his warm bed.

Suddenly he pointed to the brightest star in the sky. "Look, Figaro! It's the wishing star."

Geppetto made a wish.

"I wished that my little Pinocchio might become a real boy," he told the cat.

Geppetto fell asleep and dreamed about having a real, live son.

Well, I didn't fall asleep. So I saw the Blue Fairy fly
in through the window! She waved her wand . . .

. . . and Pinocchio came to life!

"Am I a *real* boy?" he asked.

The Blue Fairy shook her head. "If you are good, one day you will be a real boy."

"How will he know how to be good?" I asked.

"You will help him," the Blue Fairy replied.

That's how I became Pinocchio's conscience.

Pinocchio was very happy.
He could walk and talk just like a
real boy. In fact, he made so much
noise that he woke up Geppetto.

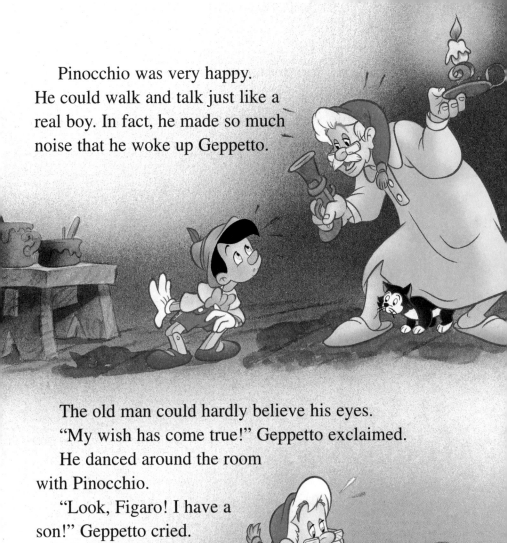

The old man could hardly believe his eyes.
"My wish has come true!" Geppetto exclaimed.
He danced around the room
with Pinocchio.
"Look, Figaro! I have a
son!" Geppetto cried.
Geppetto loved Pinocchio
as he would have loved a
real boy.

The next morning Geppetto sent Pinocchio
off to school.

Pinocchio was very excited. He couldn't wait to
learn like the real children.

Two rascals saw Pinocchio walking to school.
One was a sly fox named Honest John.
But Honest John was not honest at all.
The other was a mean cat called Gideon.
Honest John exclaimed, "A puppet who moves
without strings! We can make a fortune out of him."
Gideon agreed.

The fox and the cat told Pinocchio
to come with them.

Honest John said, "You will be the star of
Stromboli's puppet show."

"But I have to go to school," Pinocchio replied.

"Actors don't need school.
Come with us. We'll show you
the easy road to success,"
the sly fox promised.

So Pinocchio went with Honest John and Gideon.

I spent the day looking for Pinocchio.

I finally found him at Stromboli's puppet show.

The show was just starting.

"Ladi*eees* and gentlemen!" Stromboli announced.

"Presenting the one and only puppet without strings!"

Pinocchio came out
onto the stage.

He sang a
funny song.

He danced with the
other puppets.

The crowd clapped and threw gold coins.
Pinocchio was a star!
I thought Pinocchio didn't need me any longer.

But I was wrong!

Stromboli wouldn't let Pinocchio go home to Geppetto. Instead he locked poor Pinocchio in a cage.

"You're going to make lots of money for me," the greedy Stromboli told him.

I saw Stromboli
driving his wagon
out of town. So
I decided to say
good-bye to
Pinocchio. I
found my friend
in the cage.

He was crying. He was sorry he hadn't gone to school. And he wanted to go home.

I tried to set Pinocchio free, but I couldn't open the lock.

It seemed hopeless.

Then Pinocchio saw
the wishing star.

In a twinkle, the
Blue Fairy appeared.
   She asked Pinocchio
what had happened.
   Pinocchio told her
one lie after another.
   With each lie, his
nose grew longer . . .
and longer . . .

. . . and longer!

"Tell the truth," I begged Pinocchio.

Finally he did.

The Blue Fairy smiled. She waved her wand.

Pinocchio's nose became short again. And he was free!

"Remember," said the Blue Fairy. "A boy who won't be good might as well be made of wood."

Meanwhile, Honest John and
Gideon were in a tavern.
A fat coachman was there, too.
He showed them a sack full of gold.

The coachman told
Honest John, "Collect
some bad boys who
play hooky from school
and I will give you this
sack of gold. I have a coach
leaving at midnight for a place
called Pleasure Island."

Just then Pinocchio and I were racing
home to Geppetto.

I ran very fast. I didn't see Honest John stop
Pinocchio until it was
too late.

Honest John told Pinocchio all about Pleasure Island.

"Boys play there all day and never have to go to school," the crafty fox said.

"That sounds like fun!" Pinocchio agreed.

Soon Pinocchio and a coach full of boys were headed for Pleasure Island.

I thought Pinocchio might need my help. So I jumped on the back of the coach.

We rode through the starry night. Then we sailed to Pleasure Island.

Pleasure Island was full of rides and sweets.
The boys did whatever they wanted to do.
Pinocchio made
friends with a bad boy
named Lampwick.

Lampwick smoked cigars.
He showed Pinocchio how
to play pool.
  But then something
terrible happened.

Lampwick grew donkey ears.
He grew a donkey tail. He began
to bray just like a donkey.
  Hee-haw! Hee-haw!
  Lampwick turned into
a donkey!

Pinocchio started to
laugh. But he just brayed
like a donkey.

Hee-haw! Hee-haw!

Then Pinocchio grew
donkey ears and a
donkey tail.

He was turning into
a donkey, too!

"We've got to get off
Pleasure Island before it's
too late!" I cried.

Pinocchio and I jumped
into the sea.

By the time we reached the shore, Pinocchio had stopped turning into a donkey. But he still had his long ears and tail.

We ran to Geppetto's shop. No one was home!

Pinocchio and I didn't know what to do.
Then a letter floated down from the sky.

I read the letter aloud. "Geppetto
went to look for you. His ship was
swallowed by Monstro
the Whale."

"We must save him!" Pinocchio cried.

At that moment Geppetto, Figaro, and Cleo
were inside Monstro's belly.
"We'll starve if Monstro doesn't
open his mouth soon,"
Geppetto said
to them.

Pinocchio and I
went back to the shore.
Pinocchio tied a
rock to his tail.
Then we jumped
into the sea and sank
to the bottom.

We looked all around.
A school of fish swam nearby.
We finally spotted Monstro.
The giant whale was sleeping.

Suddenly Monstro woke up.
He opened his huge mouth.
Monstro swallowed all the fish.
He swallowed Pinocchio and me, too!

Soon Pinocchio and I were in Geppetto's boat. Geppetto cried, "My son! I thought I would never see you again."

Pinocchio hugged Geppetto. He promised he would never leave his father again.

Then Geppetto saw
Pinocchio's long ears
and tail.
"What happened?"
he asked.
Pinocchio felt ashamed.
"I'll tell you later," he
said. "First we need to get
out of here."

Pinocchio had a plan.
"We need to make a fire.
The smoke will make
Monstro sneeze."

They built a big fire.

Sure enough, the huge whale opened his big mouth. "Ah . . . Ahhh . . .

. . . AH-CHOO!"
We were all blown out of Monstro's mouth.
Geppetto was too weak to swim.
"Save yourself," he told Pinocchio.

But the little wooden boy would not leave
his father. Pinocchio pulled Geppetto to shore.

Geppetto woke up and found Pinocchio lying in the water. Pinocchio didn't move at all.

Geppetto took Pinocchio home.
He put the little wooden boy on his bed.
Geppetto wept. "Good-bye, my brave son.
You gave your life to save me."

Suddenly a
bright light
shone around
Pinocchio.
His wooden
limbs changed
to real arms
and legs.

His eyes
opened.
Pinocchio
was alive.
And he was
a real boy!

Geppetto hugged Pinocchio.
They danced all around the room.
At last Geppetto's wish had come true.
Which is just what happens when you wish upon a star!